Trysts From The List

To Be Or Not To Be

Sunshyne Baker

ISBN-10: 0692253548
ISBN-13: 978-0692253540 (HoneyBee Press)

CHAPTER ONE

"The only door guaranteed to stay closed, is the one you never attempt to open."
S.W

I blame Carl and his list. Just like anything else created for the net, I know the intentions behind the concept were good. Think about it: Facebook was a great tool for alums and colleagues to keep in touch- who knew it would also be a great way to catch a partner cheating with the kid you knew back in middle school when you were going through that awkward ugly period who is now looking like some kind of supermodel? YouTube, another great invention- it allows me to find educational content for my classes, yet apparently one can learn the art of "twerking" as well or see multiple uses of the word "ratchet."

In terms of this particular classifieds site, I submit the following case in its defense: where else can you get tickets to a Sixers game (granted folks are paying people to take them off their hands these days), adopt a kitten, get a free dresser someone is planning to toss out and apply for a new job making six figures all while waiting for a response to a post you wrote in the Personals section?

It's that damn Personals section that is both the challenge and the opportunity for the site. Today my search began innocently enough. It started with a perusal of the jobs section in the hopes of finding a part time tutoring gig to supplement my income, yet inevitably my attention wandered to the section innocently labeled Personals. For anyone new to the site you have to understand it's like a whole 'nother culture over there with a strange language and protocol. Reading through some of the titles and ads, you would think you needed a translator the first time. It's not unusual to find a post with the title: Blk sub 4oral and 420 friendly, likes to ski, light BDSM m4m, m4fm- which in plain English is, "Hey I'm a guy who is cool with weed and coke (420 and skiing) looking to be dominated by another guy or a couple and yeah you can be a little rough with me." Needless to say, the posts can be a somewhat, umm, forward to put it mildly, so my first time in that part of town I was alternately confused, turned on, shocked, disgusted, intrigued and did I mention turned on? Okay- so not so much by the post above, but section labeled w4w definitely caught my eye.

I've been feeling a little naughty lately and it's been bubbling to the surface. After hot, steamy sex with my hunky caramel colored, 6'3 muscular hubby I would whisper soft thoughts of what I'd do if another woman was there in bed with us and how much I would enjoy pleasing them both. Giving voice to these fantasies adds an element of fire to our intimate moments. To his credit, he never pushes this idea, it is all me and my freaky ID rearing its nymph-like head (my Superego seems to be on sabbatical). I have always found women sexy and especially enjoyed the obligatory bisexual scenes directors would through into porn. Yet, having never gone all the way with a woman before, I really can't say what brings the idea to mind now. It's not like I am bored in my marriage or sexually unsatisfied; quite the contrary actually.

If I really think about it, I can recall getting wet on the occasion that I would share a bed with my hot college roommate. Sometimes, after a night at the club we would come back to the dorm, a large group of girls feeling giddy from flirting and teasing all night. With limited space and beds, we would inevitably end up sharing a bed. On these occasions, my roommate and I had an unspoken mutual agreement to bunk together which was supposed to platonic and innocent. As she snuggled behind me, spooning me intimately, I could feel the hardened points of her nipples on my back, her satiny smooth thighs pressed to mine and the heat of her pelvis on my ass. I can remember sensing that tickle on my clit that typically signals my arousal with a man. These feelings were confusing to me and I quickly pushed the feeling and accompanying thoughts to the back of my mind. I dismissed them because my entire dating life centered on men and the thought of being sexual with a woman was so taboo. Yet, I would lay wake with unbidden desires taking root, swirling fantasies in my mind. I can still feel her soft breaths on my neck and the urge to turn over and take her, to devour her whole body with my soft kisses. Instead, I would fall into tortured sleep, with clinched thighs at times secretly sliding my finger to my swollen clit.

With all of these memories tip toeing back around the edges of my mind and having never actually kissed a woman, despite the trend in pop culture, I find myself sitting here perusing the posts.

As I scroll down the page, I see posts such as "420 playmate wanted" and since I don't indulge in good ole mary jane I keep looking; "I want to eat some pussy" sounds intriguing but I'm feeling like I want a little more of a connection and not a random hook up; "looking 4 a BBW Pillow Princess" sounds nice because I like the idea of being considered a princess until I read it and notice that 1. I am a Beautiful Woman but not Big and 2. A pillow princess is a woman who prefers to be on the receiving end of things.

While I love to receive pleasure, I also get turned on giving it, at least with my husband. When I'm honest with myself, the fantasy I envision involves mutual satisfaction. I see her body, feminine, soft and curvy, entwined with mine in bed, passions running so high that we roll on the bed, each vying for position and trying to soak up all of the sensations.

When I come across a post in all caps that reads, "SO NO ONE WANTS TO SIT ON MY FACE???" I'm too through and I have the urge to just forget the whole thing and go to Zappos to find a good deal on some shoes (because one could argue an almost orgasmic experience finding a good deal on a sexy pair of stilettos).

Then my ID, that primal aspect of my unconscious according to Fraud, I mean Freud, whispers,

"Siaani if these other chicks can post, why don't you try? Maybe the girl of your dreams will just happen to be doing just what you're doing and will respond to you."

With a compromise, my Ego supplies the rationale, "Hey, you believe in the law of attraction, put it out in the Universe and see. No harm, no foul."

So, I get up and stretch in my yoga pants that read *Love Pink* on my curvy little booty and saunter over to pour myself a glass of Shiraz and I return to my laptop on my table to muster the courage for my first CL Post.

Writing the post is actually wrought with pressure. I mean, how does one come up with a snazzy, provocative title with just the right amount of double entendre- e.g. "It's raining let's get wet"? Then once the marketing is done with the right tag line, there's the content. I am naturally verbose and even more so with a glass of wine and as I sit at the table in my suburban eat-in kitchen

I ponder how to snare the perfect woman with my words.

I read some ads that were too brief- as in "Hey cum over and lick my pussy. I host." Then I read others that were so much like a damn novel I felt like I needed a bookmark to come back and finish it.

Then there's the question- to include a picture or not? I'm a high school English teacher so including a face picture could mean the end of my career. There was a news story out recently involving students getting access to a teacher's risqué pictures. Yet, I know something about marketing and I know posts with pictures stand out.

My eye is drawn to a post that has a picture included and I decide to click on it. To my utter amazement, I see a photo of the world's largest zoomed in photo of a woman's hairy pussy, closer than I think her gynecologist has been. I swiftly back arrow out of the page and do my best to unsee that image. Ohhhkay… perhaps no picture for me.

So, with wine lubricating my thoughts and the idea of what I'm about to do lubricating my….well you know- I begin to type my ad:

"Sexy, Mature Woman…" which I immediately delete because "mature" makes me sound like a member of AARP and I'm not nowhere near there yet, though I may be joining the MILF club reluctantly since I am in my mid 30's. I know I "still got it," although my younger sister insists that if I have to make such a proclamation then I must have lost it somewhere along the way. I am a 5'5, medium build, honey brown complexioned lady with lovely 36D perky breasts and athletic legs. As I reflect on what I have to offer I consider adding that information to my post.

By the end of my second glass of wine, I have what I think is the perfect post:

"Sexy Teacher Looking to Learn a Thing Or Two: Hi Ladies, I am new to this so be gentle (but not too gentle). Lately, even though I'm married, I have been thinking about what it would feel like to have my smooth, silky legs wrapped around another woman's body. To feel the soft caress of her finger tips on my skin and the tip of her tongue on my nipples while I explore her body with my full lips. I'm sure you get the picture ☺ Me: African American, petite, nice eyes, pretty smile, cute round

booty, shoulder length naturally curly hair. My Match: Sexy with a capital S! Please feel free to respond with a picture and a little information about yourself."

I realize I need an email address that can be used for these freaky responses. I rapidly create: mzsexyteach and publish my post. There done.

The anticipation of what I'm about to do turns me on and just in time too because my handsome mister comes in from the 11am-7pm shift. I close my lap top as he enters the kitchen and I see the smile that crosses his face and it lights up the whole room. It's the smile that I have seen for the last 10 years that makes my heart flutter. He's a hip hop guy all grown up with the perfect shaped lips like LL Cool J framed by a sexy goatee- think Common or Joe Budden. The mixture of his swagger and his intelligence is a heady combination. It's the best possible result of a tough upbringing in a part of Philly aptly and affectionately called "The Bottom" by its residents. He made it through all the stereotypic ghetto horror stories to go on to college on a track scholarship to study information technology.

I stand and walk into his embrace, feeling his muscular arms wrap around my whole body and he kisses the top of my forehead in greeting. I stand on my tip toes and tilt my head for a proper kiss. As our lips meet I feel the yearning and desire that I have for him that lays just beneath the surface ready for ignition.

He murmurs teasingly, "Mmm, I see you opened that bottle of Shiraz. What you up to?"

I respond, "That's for discussion later. For now, it's Friday night and I wanna get laid. Follow me upstairs."

Surprised at my uncommon forwardness, he responds "Bet. You ain't said nothing but a word sexy." Our banter is always like this- a little 'hood,' a little playful, a little sarcastic and very flirty.

I turn and take the stairs with just a hint of extra sway in my hips and I can hear him making appreciative sounds behind me. We go into the bathroom and as he begins to undress I am distracted by his form, his golden skin tone and handsome angular face.

I turn on the mp3 player and select one of our favorite Pandora Stations. He states, "That Sade can never go out of style," as her sultry voice fills the room.

Once undressed, we step into the shower and embrace under the spray of the rainforest nozzles. We have a large bathroom, a must have for our dream home knowing how we enjoy showering together. It is a beautiful mixture of gray and blue hues, fully tiled encased in glass with a shower head on each end. For the occasional bubble bath, there is a deep and extra-long (because of his height), Jacuzzi tub on the opposite end of the room. The music surrounds us from the speakers we had installed in the ceiling and we kiss passionately. His lips are the lips I fantasized about as a young teen practicing kissing and wanting to do it the right way.

I break the kiss to say, "You would think we didn't just see each other this morning."

He replies, "I didn't get none this morning." I laugh softly and kiss his smooth chest.

He's meticulous with his grooming, always shaving everywhere, which I appreciate. I decide to show my appreciation now by dipping my head lower to his abdomen and I receive a little poke to my chin from his happy buddy.

"My bad," he says to which I respond, "Mmhm you meant to do that, I know what you want."

I slowly wrap my thick lips around his member. He's almost too much to take and I have to ease back as the water cascades around my neck and body. I suck him, gently at first then more assertively feeling the fullness of him in my mouth. I stop knowing that it's time; feeling that it's time and that I have to have him inside me NOW. I turn around and lean my hands against the wall, the warm water flowing down my arched back, while he enters me. Here, now, there is no gentleness and I don't want it. I want, I NEED to be fucked!

I arch more and he grabs my waist murmuring, "Damn baby, you feel so good. I've been waiting all day for this. For you." He thrusts long and deep. It's as if I can feel him in my soul. His dick is like a gift my body loves to receive.

"Yess, Yess, more please. Harder," I urge, wanting him to fill me up with his love. Then I feel my own climax building…it's coming… and all of a sudden I have an unbidden image of the two of us in the shower with a beautiful Gabrielle Union looking chick in front of me kissing me while he is behind me and that is enough to send me over the edge.

Minutes later, sated and happy we joke around and playfully splash water. My hair is soaked and I state, "You know you lucky I decided to go natural and just let this mess be curly because back in the day when it was relaxed, we woulda had to do that with my shower cap on and you know that's not even sexy."

He responded, "I know that's right."

I splash him again joking, "You not right, you not supposed to agree with me fool!"

He comments, "You know I love you whether you are wearing a shower cap or one of those ugly MaDea housecoats Tyler Perry be wearin.'"

We both laugh and he asks as we begin to dry off, "But seriously babe, what got into you tonight?"

It's at this point where I proceed to tell him more about my fantasies involving the two of us and another woman. I am shy as I share this deepest secret because I rarely share my erotic desires in this level of detail. I tell him that since I've never done it before, I really believe I have to try it on my own first.

When we go into the bedroom I use his iPad to show him the post. Rather than flipping out that I advertised my fantasy online, he responds with logic and calm which really shouldn't surprise me. It's one of the reasons I fell in love with him to begin with.

"Are you sure you're ok with this Mike?"

"Look of course it's every man's fantasy to be with two women but the bottom line is I want you to be happy. This is a big step for us. If you need to test this out on your own before we go any further then just be safe and keep me posted."

I was kinda dumbstruck by his answer. I viewed so many posts tonight of women stating, "Must be discreet. My husband doesn't know." It felt good that I didn't have to hide these desires but I didn't have to physically share them right away either.

With that, he was ready for round two. Needless to say we ended up with cereal for dinner that night.

CHAPTER TWO

I woke early Saturday ready to do my morning gym routine. I text my gym buddy, Tiffany.

Siaani: Gm girl. U know wht time it is. Let's get ta gittin.

Tiffany: You know I've been awake since like 6 am. You're the one tht likes to sleep late!

Siaani: That's bc I usually have sum1 keeping me up late nights..lol unlike your celibate behind. C u there! Btw got something to tell ya..I've been a bad girl!

Tiffany: You? Bad? Can't wait to hear. C u there!

As I park my silver 328i hardtop convertible in the gym's lot, I'm tempted to grab my iPhone and check to see if I have any replies to my post. I look at the clock realizing its five minutes until class and this instructor does NOT play so I push the idea to the back of my mind.

I walk in and Tiffany is already standing in our usual spot warming up. The ladies in this Zumba class are very territorial about being in their usual space, just like back in grade school gym class when we all had to stand on an assigned position, so I've learned that it's best to get there early.

"Soooo, what's up? What's the big news?," Tiffany asked.

I walk up to my friend and I whisper, "Not here. I don't wanna give old Mrs. Rosenthal over there a heart attack if she over hears."

"Ha! If it's that juicy maybe it will clear out some of the cob webs she's got down there," Tiffany retorts while gyrating her pelvis.

"Girl you so crazy!" I exclaim as I give her a light shove.

We laugh and I take my spot. Tiff and I became fast friends when I joined the local gym and started taking Zumba classes. From day one, I made it a point to spot the one person in the class who looked like she knew what she doing and was having fun. That first day I stood next to her trying to follow the tiny, super hype instructor in the front of the room, I remember turning to Tiffany inquiring, "Is she always like this?"

Tiffany replied in a low voice, slightly out of breath, "Nope. Usually it's worse. I think she slowed down because there's a couple of new people here."

"Sheesh. I dunno about this," I mumbled.

"Don't give up, " Tiffany encouraged. "You'll catch on."

From that moment we clicked and she's become one of my best friends. Now, I glanced at her athletic frame noting that she looked great in her black spandex shorts and red racerback top, with her brunette hair pulled back in a pony tail and looking still slightly tanned from the summer, though I'm sure her Italian and Latin ethnic background also added brown tones to her otherwise fair complexion.

"Ok ladies, keep it up! Let me see that energy! Raggeton! Let's go!" the instructor yelled from the front of the room as her compact muscular body moved to the rapid beat of the music.

"I swear, I don't know why I torture myself like this," I complained breathlessly.

"Because you got that tiny dress hanging in your closet that you are saving for when you lose just a lil more weight," she says as she pinches her fingers to show just this close.

"I don't know about that now. I think I saw one of those grown behind girls I teach wearing that same dress to the Jr. Prom last year which means my old ass has no business wearing it to the club."

She starts to respond but is cut off by the instructor shouting, "Less talking, more movement. Let's go!" We both roll our eyes but get into the next Pitbull song playing.

As we walk to the locker room to shower we laugh catching up on our work week. Meanwhile, I notice a slight change in my perception. I am looking around at the other women in the gym and I find myself wondering who else is harboring a secret like mine? Would the petite attractive blonde haired woman undressing next to me have thoughts about kissing me? What would it be like if I walked into the sauna and found a sexy lady, clad only in her towel, flirting with me? These questions had me wet while I showered and it wasn't just coming from the pulse of the water. What was it with me and showers?

"So, here's the post." I concluded as I pulled out my phone and opened the website. Tiff and I routinely share brunch after our workouts. We sat in the local dinner eating fruit and omelets and I quietly shared all the events from the previous day.

"You mean to tell me you never tried it in college?" She asked incredulously.

"No. You know I was raised in the church and there are all kinds of admonitions about that kind of behavior. So, when I felt a slight attraction to my college roommate I just shoved it in the back of my mind and thought 'That's some mess those white sorority girls do'..no offense."

"None taken because I WAS one of those white sorority girls who had a lil girl on girl fun," Tiff said with a mouth full of melon. "It was mainly something I did while partying or just to mess with the guys on campus. You know kissing a sexy chick just to get a reaction from them. It was all in good fun."

"Yes but did you ever go all the way?"

"What do you mean all the way? Like eating her out?" She laughed.

"Umm, yeah" I said in a 'no-duh' kind of way.

"Well yeah I had this one chick I hooked up with when I was in between boyfriends. She was so sexy and had the prettiest pussy I had ever seen."

At that comment I almost choked on my orange juice. "Wh-what??" I never considered that a woman's nether regions could be qualified in terms of beauty. I just thought it's anatomy.

She raised an eye brow and said, "I'm sure you know after looking through some of those posts with pictures not every pussy is pretty. Some look like a malformed, misshaped, Jim Henson reject Muppet- and not a cute one like Miss Piggy- I mean one like Grover or Animal." At that we are cracking up at the table as if the plain old orange juice we were drinking was a mimosa instead. Tiffany is just too funny.

"See this is why I picked you to tell. You are a whole mess" I tease. "So, tell me what happened?"

"Well, like I said, we hooked up a lot. She lived in the sorority house with me. We were both Lamda Mu's. Anyway, her name was Consuela- she and her family immigrated from Guatemala when she was 5- but I digress, so Connie had this long, jet black gorgeous hair, a lovely sandy brown complexion and the most kissable tiny lips. But like I said it was her pussy that had me mesmerized. One night in her room, our playing around went from kissing to massaging our clits. I'll never forget when we decided to remove our lacy panties all the way because up until then we had just kinda moved them to the side to finger each other. When she took hers off, I just like, melted. I mean, sure I was a little drunk because we had just left a party but I felt like there should be some kind of halo around it, it was so pretty. She waxed so she was mostly bare, with the smallest 'landing strip' giving directions to my mouth. They had to be the plumpest lips and when she laid back and opened her legs to let me taste…Mmm Mmm good like Campbell's Soup! So, yeah she and I hooked up from the time I pledged Lamda in sophomore year until we graduated. As a matter of fact, I just saw on Facebook that she went back to Guatemala to help build schools. So, yeah I can see why you wanna do this."

Her tale left me astonished. We talked more about her experiences and what I hoped to do. Meanwhile, I was so glad we had our usual booth in the corner of the diner where no one could hear our conversation though we didn't have our usual server. Instead, we had someone named Lucretia who had the raps and was overly attentive coming back over every 5 minutes to ask if we needed anything else and wanted to join in on bits and pieces of the conversation. For example, she came over when Tiff mentioned sorority parties and Lucretia decided that was a great time to share about her partying days in the 80's when she was Madonna's groupie. Talk about T.M.I.

"Let's look to see if you got any replies," Tiff suggested as we got ready to pay our check.

I assented and pulled my phone out of my purse. We went to yahoo and puzzled she asked, "Mzsexyteach?"

"Yeah don't tease. I needed an email address just for this. You know I have to be really careful."

"Oh yeah, ok makes sense." We both tilted our heads towards the phone and I gasped in surprise. In my brand new account there were 30 emails, all in less than 24 hours.

"Open one!" she urged.

"Umm ok, wait what IS all this? Let's try the one on top." The very first email had the subject line, "I'm Wat U Lookin For."

"Oh lawd, this is already suspect. You know as an English teacher this is going to get on my nerves. I mean, you know I relax my conversational speech and I have an appreciation for the utility of slang and Ebonics but come on."

"Maybe that's just her way of using short hand. Let's see what she has to say," Tiff prompted.

We opened it up to find:

"Hey boo, I like ur add. We got alot in common because I like hot sex to. You gonna like me cause I'm sexy and I got a tongue ring so you no its on an poppin. You said you in your 30's and im 25 so even tho you a little older then I like, I will give you a chance cause you sound cool. Here go my pic and my number.
Call me.
Shay-Shay"

"See! I told you," I exclaimed, "This is some bull. I'm probably too old to be doing this mess."

"Granted, that was not the best match for you. I know you were grading every typo and grammatical error as you read it."

"Yeah, she should be looking for a tutor to review her understanding of homophones not a lover," I exclaim. "I mean seriously, how hard is it to know the difference between too and to?"

"We can just delete that one. Let me pick the next one to open. Hmmm ok the 5th one down. That looks promising. The subject line is 'I like Sexy Teachers.'"

"hey how are you? hows the weekend treating ya? im from princeton, run an IT division at a firm, really easy going. any good plans for today?"

Underneath the reply was a picture of a white male, about 35 years old in a bar sticking his tongue out like in those old "Wassssp" advertisements.

"Wait, did you post in the right section?" Tiff asked.

"Yeah, I posted under women for women aka w4w so I don't know why this dude responded. And, can I just ask why these people are writing like English isn't their first language?"

"Oh, maybe you have to be more specific in your next post."

"Next post?? It ain't gon be no next post," I said with some irritation.

"See you're starting to sound like them already," She joked.

"I don't even know if I want to go through the rest of these. It's probably just people playing games."

"You never know, there could be a diamond in the rough," Tiff said hopefully.

As we stood up and grabbed our coats I stated, "Shoot, I'll be lucky if I can just get an email where someone knows 5th grade grammar."

CHAPTER THREE

The rest of the weekend flew by with Mike and me running errands and doing traditional hubby-wifey stuff. We had our weekly "Date Day" this time on Sunday and decided to Netflix the Denzel movie where he played an alcoholic pilot which actually was too heavy for a date and left me feeling like I needed damn drink myself.

We settled on running out for dessert and a walk around the nearby lake. As I licked my creamy cone, Mike asked about my post and I told him about the mailbox full of ridiculousness. Out of 30 emails only one seemed like a possibility but I was leery, based on- 1. the fact that her husband did not know she was bisexual and 2. she was vague about her physical description.

Her email simply read,
"Hi, are you still looking for a friend to hangout with? I'm a 35 year old half black half Dominican attractive fem in search of a hangout buddy. My husband does not know I'm bi and I want to keep it that way. I'm 5'5 and wear a size 10. Looking for just discreet fun, no strings attached."

"So, she sounds cute. What's the problem," Mike asked.

"The problem," I said sarcastically, "is that I don't need her man tracking us down at a restaurant or at a hotel, if we get that far, like on an episode of Cheaters."

He laughed and said, "Yeah, I can see your concern. You need me to come to your first meeting as security?"

"Aww you so sweet. But, I'm no Beyonce' so I don't need a body guard. I'll just be sure to meet her in a public place, IF we decide to meet. I'll also be sure to let you know the place and time. I don't want to freak her out thinking I'm trying to set her up for a threesome if she sees you."

"Well, aren't you sorta setting her up? Isn't your final goal a three some?"

"No!" I said a little too emphatically to be believable. "I mean I *think* my ultimate fantasy is to experience having the pleasure of you with a beautiful woman. But so far, I don't even know if I like anything beyond kissing. I gotta take baby steps, you know?"

"I see what you mean," Mike said reasonably. "Are you going to tell whomever you select that that may be your goal?"

"I honestly don't know. I want to be straight forward but how can I when I don't know myself?"

"I know something you DO know a lot about though," he said lasciviously wiggling his eyebrows in that overly-suggestive-hubba-hubba manner.

"Dude you are a straight nypho!" I exclaimed and smiled. "Didn't I just hook you up Friday?"

"Hey, that was like 2 nights ago, which in man time is like two weeks and I'm a virile man" he laughed.

"Ok" I acquiesced then I had the bright idea to add, "but this time, I want a massage after we do it and you have to use warm oil."

"I got your warm oil right here."

"Eww Mike! Dag you are so silly, I swear." I say in mock offense.

"Ok I got you. A nice massage with warm oil," he agreed.

We arrived home and showered together again, this time saving the hanky panky for the bed. Somehow, the non-sexual nature of the shower made it that much more sensual. He washed my honey brown skin gently with my favorite body scrub and took his time with every square inch. In turn, I used my soft delicate hands to caress his muscular back and I took liberty with his tight, firm round booty. Boy, does this dude have an ass like a quarter back. He chose to exit early and I stayed to enjoy the warmth of the water cascading over my skin.

When I got out and entered our bedroom Mike had lit some candles and had that old school Teddy Pendergrass playing that I like. I heard him singing, "Comon and go with me. Come on over to my place."

I walked over to him, a small smile curving my lips and my eyes flirting and stood on my tip toes to kiss him. In one swift motion, he lifted me onto the bed and I was on my back, naked skin glowing in the candle light looking up at him. He climbed onto the bed straddling me and he stated, "I decided you'll get your massage first because you have a way of knocking me out after."

"Ok I can go for that," I agreed.

He let the warmed oil trickle from my collar bone trailing down my chest and stomach. The sensation of the warm oil and its movement on my skin was so sensual. I was fascinated by how his hands could be both strong as he massaged the oil into my breasts and yet tender as he caressed my nipples until they stood erect like little Hershey kisses. He deliberately skipped my center which was growing hotter and wetter by the minute, instead moving to my legs. Each time he massaged my upper thigh, he would lightly graze my pussy with his fingertips. Teasing. Touching but not touching. It was driving me wild.

Finally, it was I who said, "Fuck the massage. You know what I want." "Yes, you told me you wanted a massage and I'm giving it to you," He replied teasingly.

"You *know* what I want," I ground out.

"Say please," he commanded.

I decided I would *not* beg so I closed my eyes. In the next instant I felt his cool lips on my thigh and making their way up. I knew that if he made it *there*, to my pulsating clit and wet pussy, I would say whatever he told me to say, that I would lose all control. His lips worked their way up to mine and he parted them with his tongue and kissed my clit tenderly. I delighted in the feeling of his lips there, of his tongue tasting me and I felt my temperature literally rising. I could feel the heat travel up my body as I moaned my pleasure.

"Damn boy, I want you so bad," I murmured.

He stopped just for a moment and looked up at me from between my creamy thighs and the sight of his handsome face there between my legs made me want him more.

"You know what you gotta do. Say please," he insisted.

Stubborn lady like I am, I said, "Baaby" in a pleading tone.

Unfortunately for me, obstinance is a trait he possess as well and he went right back to driving me insane with his licking and sucking. Just as I thought I couldn't take it anymore he stopped and moved over me so that we were face to face and I could feel his hardness pressing against me straining for entry, so I looked at him and said softly, "Please baby."

At that, he eased into me fitting like he was made for me, just the right length and width to make me feel like I could do this all night. And he moved, oh my god the way he moved, I tried to match him thrust for thrust and with each thrust he got deeper. He kissed my neck and when he kissed my lips I tasted myself and wondered if this is what my fantasy woman would taste like, sweet and feminine.

We went on like this, unaware of the passage of time, changing positions and enjoying the multiple thrills of the use of our mouths and sex to stimulate each other. Finally, we could not hold back any longer and we climaxed together, floating back down to earth and into a deep sleep. My last thought was he was so right to give me the massage first.

CHAPTER FOUR

"Mrs. Wright, I left my homework in my locker. Can I go get it?" asked Mariah one of my best students who also was also a tad boy crazy.

"Now you know you didn't leave your homework. You just want to go in the hallway because Jason just walked by," I replied.

I stood at my desk and informed the rest of the class, "After I collect your papers I will review this initial draft and give you feedback. Do not get discouraged if you see red ink on your paper. The first draft is a perfect time to ensure you are headed in the right direction." I saw several eyes roll. "And, don't forget to read chapter 12 and do the review questions at the end for tomorrow's homework," I announced as students in my last period class stood to depart.

"Why you always picking on me, Mrs. Wright?" Mariah asked on her way out of class.

"Because I know you play around but when you apply yourself you excel. Plus, you know I don't fall for that foolishness."

She seemed to sulk out of the door but I could see the small smile curving on her lips. I know my students secretly appreciate my tough love approach.

What a long day, I thought as I gathered my students' papers but I consoled myself with the fact that I made it through hump day and the weekend was fast approaching. I was almost a week since I created my post and the only possibility for a connection remained the vague half Dominican chick. It turns out that her name is Raquel and we exchanged a few emails back and forth. She's a real estate agent and seems cool. We even had a conversation on the phone that she had to terminate prematurely when her husband walked in the room. That part was still bugging me a little but I also understand that every person's situation is different. So, ultimately we decided to meet for drinks on Wednesday (given its appropriate nick name).

I admit I was nervous sitting in the parking lot of the TGI Friday's waiting for her arrival. This is it. She could be the one. But what if she is not? We exchanged one photo but the one she sent was dark and it was hard to make out her facial features. She had a nice voice on the phone so I was crossing my fingers it was a match. I also worried if I wore the right thing; I came straight from work but I had worn the sexiest outfit I could get away with while teaching: a black blazer paired with a v-necked Rachel Roy silk aqua color blouse and a black pencil skirt that came to just above my knees and hugged my curves. The kicker, to me anyway, was my shoes. I changed into my 6-inch Giuseppe Zanotti peep toe shoe boots which showed off my legs, the heels making my legs appear long and lean.

She was 10 minutes late and I told myself I would give her five more minutes. Just as I prepared to leave, a car pulled up next to me with a woman who appeared to look like the woman in the photo, but not quite. There was something I couldn't put my finger on and it was getting dark so I couldn't really see through the window but just then she sent a text that she was here. I stepped from my car, looking fly and feeling sexy and watched as she emerged from her vehicle.

The woman that I saw in front of me made me want to get back in my car, screeching out of the parking lot just like in the movies leaving tire tracks and smoke in my wake. The long hair I could see was obviously an old matted wig. I realized in the email exchange I never asked her how tall she was and she never volunteered that information. Now, I know why. In the words of Ms. Swan from Mad TV "She looka like a man." She was about 5'11 and even had a light mustache. She was probably told by some guy in a bar back in the day that shit was sexy but it's NOT. I think Eddie Murphy used this chick for inspiration in "Delirious" when he talked about his Aunt Bunny. Goonie freaking Goo-Goo (if you don't know this reference, take a moment to Netflix or youtube his standup routine and come back- sometimes old school pop culture says it best).

Damn, damn damn, I shook my head inwardly, how the hell am I gonna get out of this?

"Oh hey, here you are," she said as she went in for the hug greeting.

"Hey yourself," I said as I stuck out my hand for a shake pretending like I didn't know she wanted the hug. She was wearing jeans and had the nerve to have her muffin top obvious and a tight shirt meant to show off the cleavage of her 40DDs. We walk inside and I am crossing my fingers that the lights in the parking lot were playing tricks on me and that my impression will be better under the fluorescent lighting of the restaurant.

Wrong. Shit. I did not plan for this and now I wish I had let Mike come as security 'cause I sure would have faked an emergency. So we sit at the bar and Mr...err..umm I mean *Ms.* Raquel asks me what I'm drinking. I tell her just ginger ale though I feel like I need some of that old school hard liquor like Fred Sandford used to drink, some Wild Turkey or something, to make it through this evening.

"You look just like your picture," she gushed. Well you don't look a freaking thing like yours, I wanted to say but instead I said "Umm, I don't see much resemblance between you and your picture."

She said, "Yeah that was taken 4 years ago. I try not to send current pics because as a correctional officer I never know if I will encounter a former inmate I supervised."

"Wait what? I thought you said you were a Real Estate Agent?" I asked.

"Girl, who tells all their business on the internet?" she asked incredulously as if I were a moron. "I don't really give out 100% accurate information until I meet someone face to face."

Note to self: Google/Facebook/Tweet/Instagram or hire a private detective for the next person I meet. Instead of saying what I'm thinking, I inquire, "So what percentage of the information you shared with me *was* true?"

"I mean, I didn't lie. I just changed some facts and left some stuff out."

Umm that's called a lie, I say to myself. "OK, so let's start from the beginning," I suggest as I offer my hand again in mock greeting. "Hi, I'm Siaani; I'm 33 and a high school English teacher. I'm married and I don't have any children yet."

She takes my hand and shakes it saying, "Nice to meet you. I'm Rachel and I'm 45 and married. I have 4 kids and I work in corrections. I'm also a Gemini. What's your sign?"

I'm perplexed by the question because I was stuck back on the name exchange thinking, this chick didn't even give me the right name?? She said it was Raquel. And now we're talking zodiac signs?? I knew I had to figure out a way out of this situation. I was NOT attracted to her. I could tell right away from her tall gangly appearance, to the lack of attention paid on hair maintenance, to her four chin hairs that were irking me and the unibrow- I can't believe no one ever told her to wax. I could only shudder at the thought of what else was too hairy.

"…that's the type of woman I usually go for," she was in mid-sentence when I left my thoughts to rejoin the conversation. "What type of woman do you usually go for?"

"I don't know," I say distractedly, "I'm new to this."

"Ok, she says, well look around the room and tell me if there is anyone in here that you'd do."

I decide to play along and I look around. "Well that woman over there in the black v-neck sweater is sexy. She looks like she has the perfect lips to kiss. Hmm .." I ponder, "and that one over there, with the long black hair, she's a cutie. And of course our bartender with her contemporary Mohawk and athletic body" I say as I warm up to the game.

Our food comes and we talk. She actually is funny and seems like an intelligent and nice woman but I can tell sparks are not going to fly. We end the evening and walk to our cars. She alludes to wanting to sit in my car and talk but I get the feeling this is code for "make out" so I beg off with the excuse that I have to teach early in the morning. We hug good bye and I take off, probably a bit faster than I should have. As I drive away I hear my car stating, "Text from Raquel." I give the command to the program in the car to have the text read aloud.

It reads:

Raquel: Really nice 2meet u. I guess a good night kiss was 2much 2ask 4 since when I asked you ab your type, you practically pointed out any woman there besides me. I can take a hint. Thx for 2nite & hopefully we can still b cool. :/

I command Siri to text back:

Siaani: "Nice to meet you too. Too bad we had a missed connection. Take care and good luck in your search. ☺ "

When I get home, I head to our bedroom to disrobe and Mike sat on the edge of the bed, all ears and wanting to know every detail, at points literally laughing out loud, at my recount of the night's events.

"Wait, describe her appearance again?" he asks as he is laughing so hard he can barely catch his breath.

"Stop," I say as I playfully punch him in the arm, "you're supposed to be sympathetic dude."

"Okay, okay well was there anyone else you thought would be a good match?"

"Honestly, no" I respond despondently. "I think I may just let it go."

"Well, you always have me," he says as he pulls me down on the bed with him. I nuzzle his neck and think that maybe some fantasies are meant to stay just that- fantasy.

CHAPTER FIVE

A week goes by and it's a whirlwind at work because of state mandated testing. The kids are on edge and it's the last day. I find myself looking forward to the weekend and the nothing I have on my agenda. It's great sometimes to be unscheduled and to plan to veg out. It's my planning period but I'm ahead on my lesson plans so I pull out my iPad to read a book. As I scroll through the screens, I see the app for yahoo mail and I decide I should log in to delete my post and deactivate my account. I have been meaning to do both of these after I discovered the flood of spam and foolishness that made its way in my inbox.

Sighing, I enter my username and password and begin the tedious process.

"Pik me! From horneyguy69"- trash
"Lemme eat ya pussy from Stacey21"- trash
"I wanna sex you up from Jdawg215"- trash
"Are you still looking? from SilkySmooth74"- trash

--Wait, I click on that one out of curiosity. Hold up, this actually sounds normal and even too good to be true. It reads:

> *"Hello, I'm not sure if you are still looking but if you are then I think we could be a good match. I'm not as new to this as you are but I am just as selective. I'm attractive and I know it- but not conceited- I also know my flaws. Like most women I workout to maintain my figure. I'm single but I've been dating someone for a while now and I'm a business professional. I'm more of a homebody and not big into clubbing but I love to have good food at a great restaurant and to laugh. Anyway, I'll stop here in case you already found what/who you were looking for and if not, send me a message and let's see if we click! P.S. I attached my pic ☺"*

I read the email, *twice*, in disbelief that she actually sounds normal. Not only that, but she sounds like someone who is cool. I steel myself to open the attachment, not sure if I'd be more disappointed if it's a bad photo or a computer virus.

As it opens, a slow smile begins and I note that the woman in this photo is STUNNING. She is smiling and her smile is so warm and alluring I find that I'm holding my breath. The woman in the photo has a beautiful skin tone and delicate features. She looks like a model, she actually looks a lot like Halle Berry, which immediately makes me suspicious. I mean, what if this is a fake picture? But then, what if this is real? She could be the one. Before I lose my nerve, I quickly type out a reply:

"Hi Ms. Silky, Yes, I am still looking and I am so glad to get a regular email..lol. Chile you have no idea the kinds of weirdo responses my post generated. It sounds like we have a lot in common and I really like the pic you sent. I want to respond with one in turn but because of my profession I have to be careful. How about we talk on the phone and then see about exchanging more photos? Till later sexy (wink)."

I finish the email with my cell phone number and press send. For the rest of the day my thoughts are preoccupied with the possibility this represents. I was certainly drawn in by the picture and the way she expressed herself. I find confidence in general sexy and I'm discovering that it's a quality I would be drawn to in women as well. I find myself smiling and joking with my students more than usual and a slight blush grazes my cheeks, not due to Covergirl but attributed to the occasional thought I have about the possibility of this connection.

I find myself glancing at my phone throughout the faculty meeting at the end of the day. No call. No text. As I am leaving the building, chatting with co-workers the phone rings. It's an unfamiliar number and I find that my heart picks up a few beats. "Sorry guys, I gotta take this. See you tomorrow," I say as I walk towards my car and away from my colleagues.

"Hello?" I ask as I answer.

"Hey, this is Laila. You sent me your number to call in response to my response to your post." We both laugh.

"Yes, hi that's certainly one way to put it," I state. "I'm so glad you called. So, Laila, I'm Siaani, nice to meet you. I have to apologize because I'm new to this and I have no idea how to do this or where to start."

"Girl, it's cool. I'm no pro but from what little experience I have I know it's best to just have a regular convo and see where it takes us," she responds. I already see that the timbre of her voice is sexy. She seems to have a husky voice like Alicia Keys but not as deep as Mariah's.

"Ok, so tell me a little about yourself. What do you do for a living?" I ask.

"I'm an editor for a publishing firm and I work in downtown Philly but I live in Chestnut Hill. How about you?"

"I teach high school English at a charter school in north Philly and I live in Northeast Philly."

"Oh cool and you're married right?"

"Yup, been married for the last 10 years to a great guy."

"So does he know you posted?" she asked.

"Yeah we talked about it and we agreed this is a fantasy I can explore without disruption to our relationship. He's a pretty secure kinda guy so I'm lucky."

"Oh yeah that's great because the last thing I want is to meet up with you and have your husband jumping from behind bushes or something, so I'm glad that you're upfront about it."

We laugh and I ask her if she's a native of Philly and it turns out not only did we both grow up in the city but we also attended the same university in different years.

"Wait you went to Upenn too?" she asks incredulously.

"Yeah I did my undergrad at Temple and my masters there."

"Oh my god how about I did my undergrad at Temple too and I'm pursing my MBA now at the Wharton school of business."

"Did you ever have professor Lindenhoff?"

"Yeah he used to like to talk in people's faces with the breath that probably smelled worse than the junk yard fat Albert and them used to play in?"

"Girl yes! Who used to put h's on 'w' words seemingly just to blow more breath in your face?"

At that we cracked up and I could tell I liked her. I sat in my car in the faculty parking lot while we talked on the phone for about 30 minutes of all the uncanny commonalities between us. We ended the call with the agreement to talk more and schedule a face to face meeting. I drove home beaming, singing along with

Rihanna about cake and licking icing off, thinking perhaps I will experience my fantasy after all.

CHAPTER SIX

"...then she called and we talked and I'm like she sounds cool!"

Mike and I were having dinner on his one night off. "So you gonna meet her?" he asked with a mouth full of pasta.

"Yeah I'd like to. I just don't want a disappointment like last time."

"Then why don't you try to meet her asap. Call her up and see what she's up to. It's the weekend and I actually have to make a run to Home Depot."

"You always at Home Depot" I tease, "that place is like your second home. I know your second wife is that Jamaican cashier with the curly weave."

"Nah man, she's not my type but from the photo you showed me your new girlfriend might be" he raises his eyebrows suggestively.

"I gotta see for myself first so back up buddy," I say playfully.

We finish dinner and I walk into my bedroom and sit on the bed. I decide to take a chance on calling her.

She answers on the first ring, "Hey you.. Wassup?"

"Well.." I hedge, "I'm wondering if instead of delaying you'd wanna meet for drinks tonight?"

"Umm ok I'm shopping in Target right now. Let's say we meet in two hours at Chickie n Petes?"

"Ok see you then!" I say just a little too excitedly.

I can't believe how easy this was. All of a sudden I'm nervous. What if I'm not her type? What if she looks nothing like her picture? What if her personality isn't this cool?

I decide to dismiss these concerns go to my walk in closet to find what to wear. I don't want to wear something too suggestive because then I'd look "thirsty " as my students would say. I also need to show my "assets" so I decide on skinny jeans, black stiletto leather boots and a cute burgundy sweater with just enough v neck to show my "girls" off but not enough to be trashy. I style my curls, apply a little makeup making special effort to accent my full lips and almond shaped eyes.

When I arrive I decide to go to the bar rather than wait in the car like before. I'm not much of a drinker so I order a simple Cosmo and text Tiff while I wait.

Siaani: Hey chica whatcha doin?

Tiffany: Hey lady! I'm just winding down and about to watch some Lifetime movie.

Siaani: Girl, I don't know why. You know every LT movie has the same dag on plot- my bf is a stalker and I'm gonna fight back and fall in love with the guy who taught me self-defense... lol!

Tiffany: Wrong! In this one the stalker is the self-defense guy :)

Siaani: Ne way, I decided not to give up on my search so I'm waiting at the bar to meet sum1 new...I am soooo nervous after last time.

Tiffany: Wht? After that craziness last time you gonna try again?? I admire your tenacity.

Siaani: Well this seems promising. She has cool convo and the pic was a knockout so we'll see...I'm just so nervous.

Tiffany: You'll be ok. She can't be as bad as Ms. Sasquatch lol

Siaani: Wait..she jst txt that she's parking. Wish me luck!

I pull out my compact to check that my "lip gloss is poppin'" and when I look up I see someone who looks like it might be her walking in. She turns around and I have two simultaneous reactions- my heart stops and surprisingly my clit jumps. I feel an instant, visceral reaction to her. She smiles and walks over to me.

As cliché as it is, I can see where the expression comes from because her smile really did brighten the whole room. She seemed genuine as she approached me and hugged me. She is petite, with a chic, stylish haircut, and delicate features. Yet, she has an hour glass figure. Even though she wore a shirt that was modest and provided far more coverage than my own, I could see that she had beautiful perky breasts. When I hugged her she felt so soft and I had an instant image of what it would be like to hold her this way in the bed.

"Hey Miss Sexy Teacher," she says playfully.

"Well hey yourself Miss Silky," I respond with a smile.

"Wanna just sit here and talk?" she asks.

"Sure," I respond. "Man I'm so nervous, I have no idea where to begin."

At that point the bartender approaches us and she orders a Mai Tai. The banter with the bartender seems flirty and playful. I can tell he is looking at us in an appreciative manner and I think it's hot that we are there to meet to discuss having a sexual liaison and no one knows but the two of us.

The conversation just flows after that. We pick up discussion of our respective careers and family life. I discover that she spends most of her spare time volunteering with foster children, taking care of her aging mother and working out at home- she attributes her regiment of daily squats to her round booty. We laugh about that and I talk about going to Zumba with Tiffany. This leads us to talking about who in our lives knows about this aspect of our sexuality. She mentioned that while she is dating men, no one in her family besides her younger sister, knows she has also dated women. She doesn't see herself in a long term committed relationship with a woman but she knows that there is a part of her that yearns for a physical and emotional connection to a woman. I admit to her that I have no idea where I stand in this regard and I recount the story of my attraction to my college roommate.

"You mean as an adult, you've never looked at a woman in a sexual way?" she asked as she sipped her drink. While sipping, I noticed the way her lips touched the straw and her little pink tongue slipped between her lips and I couldn't help thinking about *her* in a sexual way.

My eyes sparkled and I smiled a flirty smile and responded, "Not until now."

She blushed and said, "Oh yeah? You sure you could go all the way?"

"Quite frankly, while I haven't had the full experience, this I *do* know-- I know me and I know that when I make up my mind about something then I do it. And I do it *well*," I say with emphasis. "I'm an overachiever in every sense of the word."

"Go 'head with your bad self," she says as she looks at me over the rim of her glass. We laugh and she playfully touches my leg at times. I find that I am licking my lips more than usual and biting my lower lip.

"So you know you're being a tease playing around with those sexy lips right?" she asks.

"Who me?" I respond all wide eyed and innocent. We continue the flirty banter full of double entendre and I feel the air sizzle with attraction.

It's time to leave and we walk out to the parking lot together. This time I am hoping to be asked to sit in her car to talk. She turns to me and asks if I want her to drive me to my car which is parked a few aisles over and to the rear of the lot. I tell her "Sure," and she gets in the driver's side while I open the passenger door of her new Altima. It's sleek and comfortable with a contemporary interior.

She starts the car and there's smooth jazz playing softly and I direct her to my car. She makes small talk about how she just leased the car explaining that leasing allows her to have a relatively new car every few years or so.

We pull up next my car and the sexual tension is almost palpable. I turn to tell her thanks for meeting and to wish her a good night and that is when she leans over and kisses me. That first sensation of her soft lips on mine, of the small moaning noise she made when I returned the kiss, tentatively at first then with more intensity, was pure bliss. We wrap our arms around each other and draw close but are inhibited by the angle of the seats and the design of the car. She is the most amazing kisser- knowing just how much tongue to give without being sloppy and how much pressure to apply. We explore each other and I enjoy all of the femininity of her and the taboo nature of our meeting.

"Damn chick," she murmurs breathlessly. "Ditto," I say as I pull away to get myself together.

"Sheesh, there's definitely chemistry. I guess we will talk more to see about where this leads," she says as I gather myself to get out of the car. "Yea, let's email. Ciao bella!"

During the car ride home, I am reeling with emotion and horny as hell. I can feel that I started to get wet just from her kisses. I could only imagine what it would feel like to have her all alone without any barriers. What I do know is that I need an outlet for these sexual feelings and I know just who had better be back from Home Depot to reap the benefits.

CHAPTER SEVEN

Another weekend flies by and I am feeling buoyed by the communication with Laila. She is free-spirited, funny, flirty and frisky- all of the four "F's" I am learning I would look for in this kind of situation. We text throughout the day and send emails during the week. I find myself checking my phone and my email, hitting refresh during the small breaks that I get during the day. Some emails are "pen pal-ish" talking about our days at work and getting to know each other's personal lives. I share the triumphs and challenges of teaching and she shares hilarious stories about her co-workers. In other emails we talk about our fantasies.

She shares with me about her most recent friendship of this nature that ended over a year ago. It's nice to know that they are still friends. It would be a red flag to me if it ended in some kind of drama- can we say 'pet rabbit in the pot a' la Fatal Attraction'? Old reference, I know but still one of the scariest movies when it comes to stalkers in a relationship. It's also nice to know the lady moved across the country to LA and so there's no need for me to worry about them rekindling something (I refuse to acknowledge that I want her all to myself but I kinda do).

We share our turn on and turn offs: turn ons- sexy shoes and flattering clothes; turn offs: hairy legs and underarms as well as odd odors and nail biting. We decide to go to the movies one night and yet again I want to do so much more than is possible in a theater. In the dark, I find myself grazing her thigh as I adjust the arm rest. She gives a small "mmmm" of approval and so I stroke her lightly over her black skinny jeans.

I know that I want more than these small "make out" sessions and the time is coming soon. I admonish myself to take it slow but after two weeks of this torture I know my resolve has faded.

I decide to shoot her an email:

To: SilkySmooth74@kmail.com
From: Mzsexyteach@ymail.com
Subject: I can't take it anymore!

Dear Ms. SilkyS,
I want- no I NEED- some intimate time with you. These last few weeks have been great getting to know each other. We are both grown, sexy confident women and we know what we want- Each other! So, even though I'm the newbie, I say don't hold back on my account. Let's spend some time together alone. No pressure beyond the promised pleasure of your lips on mine- the ones on my face that is.
What do you think?
xxxo
Siaani
Sent from my iPhone

No sooner than I hit Send do I get a response in my inbox:

To: Mzsexyteach@ymail.com
From: SilkySmooth74@kmail.com
Subject: Panties in a bunch

Dear Mz. Sexy,
Girl, you ain't said nothin' but a word! Do you know how many nights I have pleasured myself with thoughts of all the things I'd do to you? Even if it doesn't get as far as all of that, why don't you come over to my place- Friday night around 8pm? We can watch Love Jones since you said that's one of your favorites and just chill.
I'll be a good girl…if you want me to (wink).
xxxo
Laila
Sent from my iPhone

Smiling and feeling excited, I rapidly type out the response:

To: SilkySmooth74@kmail.com
From: Mzsexyteach@ymail.com
Subject: Now you're talking!

I will be there with a bottle of Roscato because you mentioned you like it. Is there anything else you would like me to bring?
xxxo
Siaani
Sent from my iPhone

To: Mzsexyteach@ymail.com
From: SilkySmooth74@kmail.com
Subject: You can bring...

...Just your sexy, curly headed self. I'll take care of the rest.
Kisses (all over),
Laila
Sent from my iPhone

The anticipation of the *possibility* of being more physically intimate and expressive with her had me on "ten" all week. Interestingly, it also amped up my sex-drive at home. I have been the definition of cougar, attacking Mike whenever he happened to be home. He knows that I'm scheduled to hang out with Laila but he senses that this part of the experience is just for me so we haven't really discussed it much. In fact, I haven't really talked about it much with Tiff either preferring instead to spend more time with my thoughts.

On Friday, school is closed due to teacher training and I find myself distracted by thoughts of what I could possibly be doing in just a few hours. Laila and I have been exchanging flirty texts all day; she texts me from her office and I am responding using my phone discreetly as I am shown the world's most boring PowerPoints. There should be some kind of rule against reading word for word on PowerPoints in a monotone voice. As a teacher, I am assessed and evaluated all the time for my instruction effectiveness. Why in the world these trainers do not have to conform to the same standards is beyond me.

When I glance at my messages I see that she tells me things

like how much she loves to give pleasure and how wet she gets just thinking about my kisses. I tell her how much I am looking forward to her soft caresses and how I adore the sound of her voice. The training can't end fast enough.

I decide to make an impromptu trip to Vicky's and buy something for "just in case," and something that will have me feeling sexy. To my delight, I spied some leopard print lacy boy shorts and a matching demi bra for my 36D's. Next, I stop at my favorite liquor store to purchase the wine. The cashier knows that I typically buy the light stuff with about 5% alcohol content so she makes a comment about this selection, "Planning something special tonight?" she asks. I just smile and agree. After that, I get home and shower, singing a watery duet with Janet Jackson. I dress in my new purchase and throw on a sweater dress and boots given that it's cold outside.

The ride to her house in the Chestnut Hill section of Philadelphia is rapid and pleasant. I just jump on the PA turnpike which to my delight is traffic free. I drive along signing to the music coming from my favorite Pandora radio station and in just a few songs I arrive at the 309 exit. As I make my way over to her neighborhood, I notice that I begin to have competing thoughts. I ask myself, what if I can't please her, what if I am expecting too much from tonight, what if I learn that I really am bisexual? I notice that I have a jittery feeling almost like I get when I'm next in line for the front row of a roller coaster.

When I pull up, I observe that her home is adorable just like her. She lives in a contemporary corner lot condo with a roof deck on a quiet street. I park and walk up to her door, heart pounding. I ring the doorbell and she answers. When she opens the door, she smiles that brilliant smile and any anxiety that I feel ebbs away. She is dressed casually in black yoga pants and a pink cami. I can see that she is sans bra and her nipples are making an imprint in her shirt.

"Hey chica! I'm glad you made it," she says as she closes the door behind me.

"Yeah it was an easy drive. I actually used to get my hair done at a salon around the corner before I went natural," I say by way of small talk.

"Oh ok, cool. Well, come on in and let's open that wine you

have."

Her condo is beautiful with a cathedral ceiling and is impeccably decorated. She grabs the corkscrew and we head to her sofa. She has a nice sized flat screen tv above the fireplace which is blazing.

"Your place is nice and this is good," I comment as I sip the Roscato.

"Yeah, it was a steal because I bought it at the right time in the market. I'm actually planning to pick up another property after I complete my MBA," she states as she seats herself next to me, on leg tucked underneath.

The movie is playing in the background and we are cracking up at the 90's and commenting on our love of spoken word, reciting some of the pieces in the film along with the actors. We have both seen *Love Jones* a billion times and discuss why it's a favorite. As we watch and the scene comes on where the sexual tension builds between Darius (Larenz Tate) and Nina (Nia Long) she shifts from casually stroking my leg to playing in my hair. I can't resist and I lean over to kiss her. My kiss pushes her back, with me on top feeling the warmth and fullness of her body beneath mine. The movie forgotten but with the soundtrack in the background, we explore each other's lips with increased passion, our hands also engaged in their own exploration. Our breathing becomes rapid and I'm feeling encumbered by my clothing. She whispers into my neck, "Come with me," and she grabs my hand and we head upstairs to her massive bedroom.

She has a California King bed with lovely deep navy blue sheets. We stood in her bedroom kissing and exploring and she says, "You must be hot, let me help you get this off." Laila starts at my thighs, sliding my dress up and over my head, kissing the exposed skin as it's revealed. Standing there with the glow of the candle light accenting my amber skin tone, she admired my sexy lingerie.

"I have wanted you, like this, in my bed with me, since the night we met," she states as she boldly looks into my eyes. "You are so damned gorgeous inside and out. I want to spend all night demonstrating to you what you've been missing."

For the first time I'm lost for words- me- an English teacher. Finally, I whisper, "Then do it."

At that, she shoved me back onto the bed and she straddles me. She removes her shirt and I see what I have wanted for so long. Her beautiful, perky breasts are sitting alluringly in her bra and I want to free them. She leans down to kiss me and I wrap my arms around her, unfastening the bra so that I can feel her breasts on mine. She releases my breasts from my bra as she kisses them. I feel her hot tongue on my nipple and it sends instant messages to my clit which is jumping for release. I thrust my hips upwards to meet hers and the sensation is so subtle and yet satisfying that I want more.

"Please," I find myself pleading, "I need you. I need more. Please." Having teased my breasts, she trails kisses down my abdomen to my outer thigh. All I can do is wish those kisses were where the yearning emanates, but she is taking her time, making me experience the wonderful agony of her kisses and her tongue. She makes her way to my inner thigh and I think I can't take it.

I want to feel her tongue on my clit, to feel her tongue inside me. I am moaning incoherently and pleading as she kisses my spot over my lacy panties. Then she slowly slides them down, exposing all of me and I instinctively arch towards her, wanting her face there. "You. Are. Stunning," she says looking down at me. She then slowly moves to my body and tenderly kisses me there. I can feel her tongue part my lips and I am moaning in ecstasy. Her tongue and lips are exploring me and she flicks my clit. I cry out, "Oh baby please." She uses her mouth to taste me fully and I think I can't take anymore. She moans, "Damn you taste so good," which just turns me on more. I can feel the climax building, feel it coming from deep inside.

This experience is so different than when I'm with Mike. Not better or worse- just different and I like it. I like her mouth on me and unbidden I have the image of Mike there kissing my breasts while she is between my legs and I can feel it, I tell her "Baby that's it, oh my god, that's it." I'm incoherent and close to tears when the dam bursts and I begin to shake. She kisses me one more time but I don't think I can take any more sensation there and I pull her to me. We kiss and I taste myself on her lips. I'm surprised that I like the taste and even more surprised that I want to experience everything with her.

We roll over and I feel a small sense of power on top of her looking down at her curvy, petite body glowing like warm honey. When she found time to remove the rest of her clothing, I have no idea but I like that it's just me, her and our nude bodies, breasts pressing against each other creating new sensations. I kiss her delicate neck softly and I can hear little moans of pleasure. I know, in that moment that I want to taste her, not just to "return the favor" but because I want to make her feel as good as I did. What I did not know was hearing her say my name, hearing the soft sounds of her surrender to my actions would excite me as much as if she were touching me.

I decided to follow her example and extend our playtime with teasing, tasting, caresses and fingers exploring. "Siaani, please," she begged. "I need you baby...Please" and that was it, my resolve collapsed and I dove in, with fervor wanting to please her more than any other lover before. Any worries I had about 'not doing it right' were gone because I was attuned to her body and I let her passionate cries guide my actions. "Yesssss," she cried out and began to quake. I looked up from my position between her thighs seeing the beauty of her climax as she arched her back and trembled coming again and again.

We played like that for hours, touching, teasing, tasting, whispering, and even laughing at times. It was intimate, sensual and comfortable. Laying with her after, talking softly about fantasies, desires and the future of our friendship, I felt grateful for making this connection. I felt that this is a friendship I want to grow and I felt excited about the new ways I will come know myself as a sexual being with her.

"...I've even wondered what it'd be like to have a threesome," she was saying as I lay with my head on her chest while she played in my hair.

I look up into her beautiful brown eyes and state with a sly expression, "Girlfriend, if you decide that's a fantasy you'd like to pursue one day, I just might be able to hook you up!" We laughed, rolled over and curled into each other's arms falling into blissful sleep.

CHAPTER EIGHT

"…Yeah I had a great time," I stated with my mouth full of my fluffy western omelet. I was having my weekly after workout brunch with Tiff. She wasted no time asking for details about my amorous rendezvous last night. Not one to kiss and tell, I shared just enough about my "slumber party" to have her mouth salivating for more than just our meal.

"I guess you can take your ad down now," Tiff suggests.

"Girl I did that weeks ago. After meeting her, I said to myself, 'if she's not the one then forget it.' Besides some of the responses were getting really creepy anyway."

"Creepy how?" She asked while sipping her green tea and honey.

"Well, one older man kept sending me dick pics and offering money to take me out as if I'm some kind of private escort. Granted, I was deeply offended by the shriveled up uncircumcised images of his Vienna sausage however, amounts over $2000 definitely gave a sistah pause."

Tiff almost spat out her tea on the last statement and guffawed, admonishing, "Remember we have an agreement that you would warn me before saying something that might cause that reaction" she sputtered.

"You are so silly!" She wiped her mouth and grabbed her steaming mug of tea. With narrowed eyes peering over the brim she asked, "Soooo, when do I get to meet Ms. Mystery lady? You know it's not official unless she gets my seal of approval."

"I know. I know. I already told her that you're my sister from another mister. She's looking forward to meeting you."

"I know just the thing for us ladies- a spa day!"

"Girl you know just how much I love a good spa day. Let's set that up when I get back from this teacher's conference in Seattle,"

"Oh yeah, I forgot that you have a conference to attend. You're presenting right?"

"Yes," I sighed, "on enhanced web technologies in the classroom and you know how nervous I get before these things."

"You public speakers are so funny. Here you are with a natural talent for this stuff talking about being nervous. I'm sure you're gonna knock it out of the park as usual."

"I'll just be glad when it's over. It's only three days so I'll hit you up when I get back," I stated as we grabbed the check from the table and approached the cashier.

CHAPTER NINE

"I'm so glad that you could take off work to take me to the airport. It's one less stress for me," I said as I leaned over to kiss Mike's cheek when we jumped in his SUV.

"Yeah if I know you, you started packing this morning and probably packed enough for a week even though it's only a few days," Mike said as he started the ignition.

We backed out of our driveway and I couldn't help but wonder what I might have left behind. I remarked, "Actually, I started packing last night, so there!" We laughed, and I said, "though you are right about the over packing. But part of that isn't my fault. A girl never knows how many changes of clothes and shoes she will need."

"You're gonna have to take me along with you on one of these trips one day. I could be your assistant."

"I couldn't have you working for me, you'd be the main one trying to sue me for sexual harassment!"

"It's only harassment if it's *unwanted* and I always want it from you baby."

"Mmhm, are you going to miss me, baby?" I asked coquettishly.

"Nah, I plan to invite the fellas over for a party with a gang of dancers. As a matter of fact, we'll probably have them do a twerk-off."

I smacked his arm playfully and said, "You're lucky you're driving and I have somewhere to be otherwise your ass would get it for joking like that."

"Who said it's a joke?" he asked deviously. "In all seriousness, of course I'll miss you babe."

When we arrived at Philadelphia International, Mike kissed me passionately on the lips and whispered encouraging words in my ear. I exited and prepared to board my 10am flight.

Flying always makes me a little nervous as well. Though, deep down I think I'm just a slightly neurotic kind of person in general, always worried about this little detail or that. I just thank goodness that I'm not so anxiety prone that I refuse to do things. It's just enough to keep me alert. After going through the security check point with a TSA agent, who I swear took extra long rubbing my thighs and cupping my breasts, I stopped by the newsstand for a pack of gum to prevent my ears popping on the flight. I took the opportunity to peruse the shelves stocked with novels of various genres. The educator in me wanted to pick up a non-fiction work but my inner naughty girl was drawn to literature of the more erotic variety.

I selected a book of short stories about encounters between women. Ever since I initiated my new friendship with Laila, I have been more interested in being exposed to intimacy between women- in films, in literature and even in works of art. One thing I can say is that the entire flight went faster because I had the most interesting reading material.

"In preparation of our landing, please place all tray tables up and seats in the upright positions," the model-esque Latina flight attendant instructed in her sing song voice. After the two small glasses of wine and my mind filled with mental images of sexy women engaged in all kinds of compromising positions, I couldn't wait to text Laila.

"Ladies and gentlemen, welcome to Seattle-Tacoma International Airport. There is a 3 hour difference in time zone so please remember to adjust your watches accordingly. Local time is 1:15pm and the temperature is 65 degrees. For your safety, we ask that you remain seated with your seat belt fastened until the Captain turns off the Fasten Seat Belt sign. This will indicate that we have parked at the gate and that it is safe for you to move about the cabin. You may access your electronic devices at this time."

I reached into my purse and pulled out my phone. Upon taking it off of airplane mode I checked my messages and to my delight I had one from my new friend.

Laila: Hey Miss Sexy Teach, hope your 5 hour flight wasn't too bad. If I was sitting next 2u the trip would have been super enjoyable ;)

Siaani: Hey Chica, we just landed. I can only imagine what kind of naughty business we would have gotten into under the blanket across our laps. It didn't help I was reading these short stories that got my panties all wet.

Laila: Did u slide ur slender lil fingers inside 2 relieve sum of the pressure?

Siaani: How did u guess? I was thinking ab the other night when ur tongue was there. Girl I'm getting started all over again and I'm ab to get off this plane. I'll txt you when I get settled into my hotel room.

Laila: KK. Muah!

I smiled to myself as I closed the messaging app and grabbed my carryon luggage.

"Take me to the Grand Hyatt on Pine please?" I asked the cab driver as I jumped in. I called Mike and left a voice mail for him letting him know that I was on my way to check into the hotel and reminding him not to throw any wild parties. I then settled back into the seat admiring the city skyline wondering about what it would be like to live here. Whenever I visit new cities, I am always intrigued by the individual culture of the city. It's the vibe that you get from its inhabitants concomitant with its history. For example, Philly has a definite culture with its colonial roots and city-town urbanity. A slower pace than New York, it is replete with all the challenges and strengths a populous city can bring. I associate Seattle with vegan hipsters and hardworking laborers given its ports and robust fishing industry. Of course I also think of mega companies such as Starbucks and Microsoft which reminds me to text two of my students to tell them to research their scholarships. My mind is constantly going a million miles per minute which is why I will definitely be looking forward to a day at the spa upon my return home.

The drive from the airport to the hotel is a long one and it gives me the opportunity to view the landscape. Seattle is surprisingly abounding with steep hills and as I pass Pike Street I make a mental note to find some time to walk down to Pike Place Market.

"Ok Mrs. Wright, we have your reservation right here and with your Hyatt Gold Reward points we can upgrade your room if you prefer," the petite blonde haired front desk receptionist offered.

"Yes, please. That would be great. I'd love a king with a view," I replied.

"We have that and we also have a complimentary breakfast for you. Just include this card with your check at our restaurant or with in-room dining."

Now *that* put a smile on my face. I love getting a "hook-up" and feeling special. "Why thank you so much," I replied as I accepted the packet from her.

"Conference registration is right down the hall on this floor, room Portland A." I thanked little helpful Hailey and added to my mental to do list to email a compliment about her service to her manager.

I decided to go deposit my belongings and check out my room first before going to register for the conference. The room, located on the 18th floor, had a lovely view of the Puget Sound. I hung the business casual black and white Michael Kors dress I planned to wear during my presentation and took a moment to just take in the view. I was startled by my phone vibrating on the desk and serenading me with, "That girl is poison." I *have* to change Tiffany's ring tone, I laughed to myself.

"Hey girl! How about you still have that Bell Biv Devoe song as your ring tone."

"You didn't change that yet?" she laughed. "I know why, it's because you know-" she sang, *"never trust a big butt and a smile, that girl is poisonnnn!"*

"That's why I love you, you keep me cracking up. So, I made it here and it's gorgeous."

"That's why I was calling, to make sure my home girl was safe and to wish you good luck on your presentation tomorrow."

"I'm going to go register now and go grab lunch to bring back to the room so that I can prep. Most likely, I'm going to head to bed early because a girl needs her beauty rest."

"You're pretty enough as it is but I do think you should get a good night's sleep. I, on the other hand have a hot date tonight."

I bombarded her with a rush of questions. "You do? I'm so excited, who is he? Where are you going? How did you meet him? Please don't say online."

"Nope. I met him at work actually."

"What does he do? What's his name? How old is he?"

"Slow down," she chuckled. "I'll tell all in due time. His name is Tyrone O'Hara."

"What? Are you dating a Black Leprechaun- like Katt Williams?" I interjected. It's always so easy to poke fun at her that I couldn't help it.

"I knew you would say that," she responded laughing, "and no, though he just may be magically delicious. He just happens to be bi-racial with a Jamaican mom and an Irish dad."

"So, which department does he work in?" I inquired.

"Well, technically" she paused for a beat and continued, "he kinda doesn't actually, fully, all the way, work there," she stalled sounding like a nervous teen. Then all in a rush she said, "He's the UPS guy and he has been delivering my packages for the last year and before you can say anything, no making any jokes about his "package." I already know where your mind is headed."

"Well you know it's all about those little brown shorts. Those shorts leave nothing to the imagination," I teased. "Ok, ok, I'll lay off. I'm happy for you and I do not care if he's a mail man, trash man or super man as long as he's good to you."

"You should see how he looks," she gushed. "He's about 6'1, 195, all muscles, must be from all that heavy lifting, curly brown hair and green eyes girl! Green eyes!," she exclaimed.

"What, do you mean like Jesse Williams the sexy Black doctor on Grey's Anatomy?"

"Yessss, girl exactly like him. I hoped he would ask me out but quite frankly I wasn't sure I am his type. Well, today he came into my office to bring my typical Monday delivery. We had our usual flirty banter about our weekends and lack of social life when he just suggested out of nowhere that we 'grab a bite to eat' after work. I am soooo excited. I know I sound like some kind of high school girl with a crush."

"I'd at least give your reaction college freshman status," I said sarcastically.

"Oh hush, just be happy for me."

"You know I am. I want to hear all about it tomorrow after my presentation. I'm about to go let these people know that I'm here though I seriously wish I could back out now."

"You'll be fine I know it. You know what they say about

imagining the audience in their underwear? Well don't do that because your silly butt will just end up giggling through the whole thing unless there are hot women in the audience, but who knows that could be equally as distracting."

"You are too much, Tiff. Love you girl."

"Love you too girlfriend. Later."

We disconnected the call and I smiled at my friend's fortune. I hoped her date turned out as good as mine was last Friday. I smiled to myself at the memory and decided I would text Laila before bed to send her a good night kiss.

CHAPTER TEN

The hotel was packed with teachers. Everywhere I walked I recognized educators by their various disciplines. The neatly dressed math teachers, the disheveled history teachers, the preppy English teachers- though I don't think I fall into that category. I'm more in the other groupings according to generation. There are the old school teachers who wear skirts pass the knee and frumpy cardigans and on the opposite end of the spectrum there are the neophyte teachers who just finished grad school and are fresh faced ready to change the world. These would be the teachers who sometimes are hard to discern from the students with their skinny jeans, tattoos and piercings. My generation is more in-between those two extremes. In the classroom, we dress business casual but chic.

"Ok Mrs. Wright here's your packet. There's been some excitement about your presentation. Good luck tomorrow," said the kindly, white haired woman volunteering at the conference registration table. She reminded me of my grandmother, smooth mocha skin tone and a brilliant smile. I could tell that she was the kind of teacher who nurtured her students.

"Thank you very much, I'm going to try my best."

"Don't go in there thinking nothing about no 'try.' You go in there and do like Nike said and 'Just do it.'

I laughed and said, "You're right. I'll put positivity out in the universe."

"That's the attitude. I'll be in your session tomorrow too," she assured me with a smile.

"I'll look for you," I said smiling in return grateful for the support.

I took my packet and stopped in the upscale deli and picked up some lunch. I took the elevator to my room and decided I needed to work out some of the sexual tension from earlier so I stowed my lunch in the small refrigerator. I changed into my work out clothes secretly thinking that I was right to over pack and headed to the fitness center. Thirty minutes on the elliptical and what I call my triple 3's, consisting of three sets of 30 squats, sit-ups and leg lifts, I headed back to my room anxious for the shower that I so desperately needed.

I disrobed and turned the water on, grabbing my body scrub. As I stood under the spray I felt all of the soreness drain from my muscles as of being washed away. I hummed a little tune to myself thinking of that old school Tweet song, "Oops Oh My" as I began to lather my body with my hands. It felt good to caress my neck, to run my slender finger tips from my ears to trace my collarbone. Loving the smooth buttery softness of my skin as I glide my hand to my breasts, feeling the suds on my nipples and the water flowing down my body.

Without realizing it, I find my index finger between my lips, slowly circling my clit as it swelled beneath the spray. Eyes closed, head tilted back, I imagined what it would be like to shower with Laila. To feel her breasts on mine, soapy and slippery. Nipples teasing and taunting, holding each other under the water. Before I knew it, my hand became her hand and she was touching me, urging me on to higher heights and as I reached the top I called out, bracing my hand on the wall for support, breathing hard and laughing softly to myself.

Now, I can dig out that sandwich and review for my presentation.

CHAPTER ELEVEN

"Babe, there are so many teachers here, it makes me wonder who is in the schools teaching our kids," I said to Mike between bites of my honey turkey and Swiss cheese sandwich.

"You know it's hard to hear you over the phone with your mouth full right?" he teased.

"Yeah, yeah that's my bad. I just wanted to say good night because I know it's late over there. I'm feeling more confident about tomorrow as I review these slides." I was sitting cross legged in my satiny pj's and black cami, in the middle of what felt like a bed of clouds.

"You always rock at these things. I'm so proud of you whenever I hear you speak- except for when you are talking with food in your mouth," he said. It is our tradition to Skype when one of us is away on business so that we can see each other.

"Ok Jokey smurf. I just finished my 'linner' anyway."

"Linner?" He asked puzzled, raising an eyebrow.

"Yes, it's like brunch, except it's lunch and dinner, so linner."

"You stay making up words. So, have you heard from your new friend, what's her name, Lisa? Leah?"

"You play too much; you know her name is Laila. But, to answer your question, surprisingly no I haven't heard from her. I texted her when I landed and we chatted a bit. I told her I would text her again before bed and I did. I sent her a couple of messages and even left her a voicemail but so far no response."

"Don't read too much into it baby, she might just be busy," Mike suggested.

"I'm trying not to but it's weird because we have been in regular communication, since…well, you know."

"Give her some time. I'm sure she will reach out before your presentation tomorrow. Anyway, let me get back to the wild orgy I'm having, oops I mean get ready for bed."

"You are a serious clown, you know that?"

"But, I'm your clown," he said in his sly way.

"Yes, yes you are."

"...Recent research suggests that our students are eager to use technology more in the classroom. The same research indicates that we aren't using it because we are under trained. Hopefully, with some of the tools I shared with you today, you will go back to your respective classrooms fired up and ready to bring education into the 21st century. Thank you for your time and attention today."

I smiled as I walked toward the projector to turn it off and received a very gratifying round of applause. The room was filled with every seat taken. After the workshop, several attendees stepped forward to ask questions about the techniques and sites I suggested. I even noticed Mrs. Chandler, the kindly older woman from registration in the room just as she said she would be. When I felt even the slightest bit nervous during the workshop she would nod encouragingly. At one point I expected her to yell out, "Amen!" like the older mothers in the church used to do.

On a high, as I was leaving the space, I texted my crew, Mike, Tiff and Laila, to tell them how things went. Not surprisingly, Mike text back, "That's what I'm talking about!" and Tiff texted a sentence of emojis with hearts, hands clapping and raised in praise as well as little kisses. I guessed that was congratulations enough and smiled to myself. I was heading back to my room to change to take the walk down to Pike Place.

I texted Laila:
Siaani: Hey girl, it went really well today. I was hoping we could chat a   little. Where have you been? Is everything ok?

No response. Unfortunately, she didn't have an iPhone so I couldn't see if she read the message or not. It would be horrible if she were sick or if something bad happened to her. I was starting to be concerned. Always one to give people the benefit of the doubt, I decided to email her later tonight before bed in the event that something happened with her phone. Who knows, I thought, maybe she misplaced her phone and can only access email?

Deciding to make the most of the rest of my day before the late afternoon session of workshops, I changed into my skinny jeans and a cute button up white blouse, leaving the top two buttons undone showing just the right amount of cleavage. My walk to the market took me past Macy's which led to an impromptu shopping trip which, I rationalized, was totally not my fault. Nobody told them to put a Macy's between me and my destination. I picked up some new shoes (because a girl can never have too many shoes), some sexy intimate apparel and three bracelets- one for me, one for Tiff and one for Laila.

The market turned out to be well worth the walk. I took some time to enjoy a tall, Caramel Macchiato from the site of the first Starbucks. As the barista completed my order, I smiled to myself realizing with my Starbucks addiction, this was the equivalence of a personal coffee pilgrimage. Aside from the spectacle of the flying fish over the counters, there were many talented vendors selling their crafts in the market. It reminded me of a larger Reading Terminal which we have back home. I ended up purchasing a painting of the silhouette of a woman's body, curved and sleek. In the ultimate tourist move, I deposited some of my loose change in the market's mascot bronzed piggy bank, a massive pig interestingly named Rachel.

I made it back just in time for the 3pm session about reinventing the college application essay. I definitely needed this information for my juniors and seniors this year so I was super attentive despite being a little tired. I was invited out by colleagues for dinner at the Ruth's Chris Steakhouse which was conveniently located inside the hotel. I begged off though, excited to get back to my room to shower, order room service and settle down with a good book. I technically only had one more night to enjoy the hotel because the conference was scheduled to end the next evening and I planned to leave for my flight at 4pm.

Another refreshing shower, sans the solo intimacy this time, I settled into bed waiting for my room service to arrive. I had on a different cute little nighty set, this one was magenta satin shorts and a black lace cami. My hair was pulled into a ballerina bun on top of my head and I wore my black rimmed school teacher's glasses. Eagerly awaiting my order, I muted the television since they were showing a re-run episode of "Naked and Afraid." I found myself wondering what in the world would make these people think they could run around some desolate and dangerous place without shoes. I chuckled softly at the idea that my primary concern for the contestants involved foot apparel and not actual apparel.

I decided to pick up my anthology of erotica to continue where I left off on the plane. I had absolutely no business reading this now knowing that it might just leave me more sexually frustrated than anything else. Getting lost in a story about a female CEO in a bidding war with a strong competitor who happens to be an equally sexy and savvy business woman, I heard a knock at the door.

"Finally, it's about time, I was starving," I mumbled to myself jumping up to get the order. On the TV I could see that commercial with Tina Fey calling the feeling of being simultaneously hungry and irritable, 'Hangry,' which I certainly was at this point.

I opened the door with a forced smile, determined not to take out my 'hangry' mood on the server.

Standing there in a three quarter length red trench coat was Laila! It took me a moment to recognize her, her hair was styled in cute little curls all over her petite face in a Toni Braxton kind of way and her makeup was subtle with just the barest hint of mascara and natural toned eye shadow bringing out the devilish gleam in her eyes.

The coat covered the dress she was wearing and since the coat was belted I couldn't see what it looked like. What I could see were her shoes, black Christian Louboutin stilettos that had to be five or six inches high that made the arch of her feet and the curve of her legs look like a runway model's physique. My mouth dropped open, literally dumb founded. I'm sure I was not making the most flattering face as I stood there taking in the sultry woman standing in front of me.

"Wh-what are you doing here?" I stammered.

"That wasn't quite the reaction I was going for," she stated with a wry smile. It's that smile that melts my heart. I watch when her smile begins to spread across her face, lighting her mahogany colored eyes and it's as if it touches me, some place deep inside and I realize I want her to look at me like this forever.

"Well, can I come in?" she asks boldly as she steps forward pushing the door open more. I step aside, still speechless, for the second time in our short relationship. She boldly walked in the room, hips swaying beneath the coat turning to look at me.

Closing the door, the corny, nerdy side of me emerged saying way too formally, "Sure, sure come in. May I take your coat?"

She looked at me still smiling a small smile as if sharing a private joke, saying "Sure," as she unbelted the coat dropping it to the floor and I saw that she was wearing a black lace negligee with red thongs. In that moment, I lost all composure.

"Shit, you are so fucking sexy. I just can't. I can't even put all the thoughts running through my mind into words right now."

"Well stop trying to use words. SHOW me. Come show me what you are thinking."

Walking towards her, I began taking off my shorts and while reaching for my cami, she said, "No, let me handle that."

I wrapped my arms around her and kissed her deeply. Our mouths crushed each other, desire evidenced in every smack of our lips, every touch of our tongues, exploring and searching for more yet still wanting. Obtaining but not getting, seeking and not finding, there was the push pull of desire and release that warred between us. Breast to breast, nipples touching yet not due to the barest thin barrier of our clothing; pelvis to pelvis, the throbbing and tickling of our clits had me edging her closer to the bed.

I appreciated her femininity, the softness of her skin and around every bend more and more curves. I could understand why women could be bisexual; it's appreciating dual sensations, the way one can appreciate the way water can both revive and erode; or the duality of a hot stone massage, hard yet gentle, loving extremes like sandpaper and silk both having a place and purpose. In that moment, I realized this is what I was missing. It was more than a sexual fantasy, it was an aspect of me that had yet to be discovered or fulfilled, until Laila.

We landed on the bed, me on top, my arms out stretched holding myself up above her so that I could peer in her eyes, my hair hanging around my face.

She smiled up at me and said, "I'm supposed to be the one seducing you."

"Oh you already accomplished that goal," I said with sexual tension adding a breathless quality to my voice.

Gazing down at her as she lay so vulnerable and open on the bed made me want to do whatever it took to please her, to make her feel things she never felt with anyone else man or woman. Her lips, a pale pink that glistened with the barest hint of lip gloss were silently begging for my kisses.

This time, I leaned in slowly, eyes open, and kissed her tenderly, sweetly then that insatiable desire bubbled back to the surface and we kissed more deeply. I broke the kiss, sucking just a little on her lower lip. "Usher must have been talking about you when he sang 'Good Kisser'," she said between breaths.

"Your husband has been selfishly keeping all that to himself?," she teased.

"He sure has, until you," I murmured as my lips trailed to her tiny ear lobes, my tongue teasing the tip where petite diamond studs decorated their surface. She arched her back and moaned at my delicate, teasing touch of my tongue there.

I continued, exploring, kissing the sensitive curve of her neck. Occasionally allowing the tip of my tongue to trace a small pattern, hearing her moans increasing in volume. She knotted her fists in my hair pulling me to her. I gently extracted them, though I was pleasantly surprised that I liked that from her, I grabbed her wrists holding them above her head with one hand, surprising myself in my strength. I moved ever so slowly down her body to her breasts and she arched into me, saying "yes, yes." Emboldened by her response, I dipped my mouth to the lacy fabric covering her areola. Taunting her with my lips just barely hovered above her nipple, I could see it harden. I traced it slowly with my tongue. I don't know which of us wanted the removal of barrier between us more. I yearned to taste her, to experience the feeling of her in my mouth.

Sliding the delicate fabric down in slow torture for us both, I revealed my prize taking as much of her on my mouth as I could and slowly pulling back until at last I had her nipple again in my mouth, using the tip of my tongue to play it like a flute. Repeating the act on the other side, I delighted in the thrill of taking charge as I never have before. I'm certain that she did not expect all of this from a newbie like me, but that's what she gets for showing up here, I thought to myself.

Releasing her arms, she reached for me, but I was already on the move, making my way down her body, looking up at her wickedly through hooded eye lids. I rested at the apex of her midsection and asked playfully, "you want a kiss here?"

"Yes, yes I do. Please" she begged.

"Not yet," I said decisively and moved to her creamy thighs, kissing one while caressing the other. She writhed on the bed, pleading with me to taste her, to end the torment. When it became more than even I could bear, I acquiesced and as I kissed her calves and knees. I slid her thongs off tossing them aside. The site of her, shaved and inviting was more than I could take. Moving with vampire like speed, I planted my lips, my face in the center of her where I simultaneously licked and sucked her clit. She came close to climax, moving my tongue from her clit to her opening, it moved in and out rapidly, lapping her up like the tastiest dessert from five star restaurant. "Yes, baby, yes, eat this pussy," she demanded. I was caught off guard as I felt the familiar rise of my climax, her excitement and cries of pleasure edging me closer. How was I coming when she hadn't touched me? I wondered. Yet, I did not stop. If anything, I was more tenacious wanting her orgasm to closely follow my own. "Ohhh yes, Siaani, baby I'm coming so hard," she moaned turning her head into the pillow. She pushed me back slightly as she shivered and quaked in ecstasy.

I took this time to remove my panties. I had to feel her lips on me, there. I crawled up her body, kissed her lips and then moved up further until my beautiful pussy was on her face. "Oh, shit," she exclaimed, "I created a monster!"

"Yes, you have now what are you going to do about it," I challenged? At that, snake like, she flicked her tongue over my clit and I cried out, "Oh. My. God." She then took me, as I kneeled over her, riding her face. Faster and faster, I moved and she moved, her tongue, her lips, and I slid over her until my orgasm took me over the abyss.

Later, as we showered together, she explained that when we were together last week, she took note when I told her about my conference. She said that she arrived that afternoon and had her own room booked on the tenth floor for changing purposes.

"…or in the event that you turned me away," she teased.

"Like anyone would turn away from all this jelly," I mocked singing Beyoncé's old school song while patting her curvy booty.

"Yeah, I don't think the TSA agent would have permitted me to board my flight in that get up."

"She would have if it was the same one who molested me on my way here," I said sardonically.

She said she had hoped to arrive in time to see my presentation but could not get an early flight.

"Don't worry, I have one coming up in Miami in August," I offered, "so we can do this all over again if you like."

She laughed and we talked, kissed and flirted more under the gentle spray of the water.

I never did find out what happened with my room service.

The End ....*For Now*

ABOUT THE AUTHOR

Sunshyne Baker is a native of Philadelphia though she presently resides in New Jersey with her supportive family. Considering herself a "sexy geek," she writes and performs erotic spoken word and can also frequently be found cast in local film projects or on the stage of a local community theater production. She is especially appreciative of her amazing friends who aside from providing free editing can also be found clapping and cheering in the audience of every performance or event as if it's their child's third grade music recital. She has a particular affinity for The Vagina Monologues both for the sociopolitical commentary and quite sophomorically for the repeated use of the word vagina.